THE PENGUIN QUARTET

THE PENGUIN QUARTET

by Peter Arrhenius
illustrations by Ingela Peterson

SCHOLASTIC INC.

New York Toronto London Auckland Sydney
Mexico City New Delhi Hong Kong

It was the time of year when all the penguin moms swim out to the big, big ocean, to feast on fish and have fun as only penguin moms can.

While they were away, the penguin dads watched over the eggs. Max, Miles, Herbie, Charlie, and all the other dads were as bored as penguins can be. It just wasn't much fun to stand in the snow and watch over eggs all day long.

PENGUIN PUCK

Dear Dad,
The fish are
great here!

16
SOUTH POLE

Mom / Max Penguin

"I'm fed up with this," Max complained. "Same old story every year. Stopped-up beak. Frozen wings. And ice on my poor webbed feet!"

"Maybe we can think of something new to do," Herbie suggested. "What if we went on a tour?"

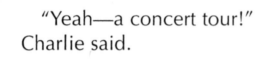

"Yeah—a concert tour!" Charlie said.

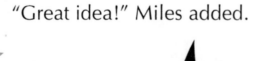

"Great idea!" Miles added.

"But what would we play?" Max grumbled. "The South Pole polka? The blizzard blues?"

"Nope," Herbie said, "we'd play the music that all cool penguins play—jazz!"

"Well, pardon me," said Max, shaking some frost from his wings, "but I'm so cool I could turn to ice—and *I* don't play jazz."

"That doesn't mean we can't." Miles tapped out a beat on the snow. "Come on, let's start jazzin'!"

"But where do people play jazz?" Charlie asked.

"In New York City," Herbie said. "In the U.S.A.!"

"That settles it," Miles said. "Let's pack our eggs and go!"

Now, you have to fly to get to the United States from the South Pole. And even though penguins have wings, they *can't* fly. So the four penguin dads had to take an airplane to New York City.

"This is awful," Max said as they boarded the plane.
"I feel like I've been swallowed by a whale."
Herbie found a pair of headphones on his seat.
He tried them on and pushed a button.
"Listen! This is jazz," he said happily. "This is
just how we're going to sound."

At last they arrived in New York. But when they went to pick up their luggage, they discovered that Charlie's egg had disappeared!

"Just what I expected." Max looked around suspiciously. "Egg thieves *everywhere*."

"I've lost my egg," Charlie sobbed. He waddled into a coffee shop and began to weep. "You haven't seen it, have you?" he asked a kind-looking lady.

"Well, someone did just drop off a very strange egg. . . . Could it be yours?"

"Yes!" Charlie shouted. "There's my little baby." He looked at the egg crossly. "Shame on you—you could have been poached!"

As the penguins walked the streets of New York, they gawked and squawked in amazement.

"Talk about big!" Herbie said.

"Yeah," Max said, "and what a smell! How could anyone possibly live here?"

"The problem isn't *how* we could live here," Miles answered. "It's *where*. I'm so tired, even the webs of my feet hurt."

"Check out those guys!" Herbie pointed at two men in fancy suits. "They look like they have someplace to stay. Let's follow them!"

The men in the fancy suits went into a large building with a sign that said, "Waldorf Astoria Hotel." Herbie asked the lady behind the counter if they could stay at Mr. Waldorf's place, too.

"Hmm . . ." The lady frowned at the penguins. "Who are you?"
"We're the Penguin Quartet," Herbie explained.
"Oh, I see," the lady said. She looked a bit more interested now. "I never knew that penguins played music. You're welcome to stay here!"

The lady opened a door, and the penguins waddled into the largest room they had ever seen.

"Now this is the way to live!" Miles said through a mouthful of fish. "It was awfully nice of Mr. Waldorf to leave us a snack."

"We'll have to be sure to thank him," Max agreed.

That evening, the penguins went to look for a jazz club. "I'm homesick," Max grumbled. "I want to go back to the South Pole, where the air is clean and the fish are fresh."

"But we can sit around at home anytime," Miles said. "This is so much more *exciting*."

Herbie spotted a man standing in a stairway. He looked furious. "I can't believe this!" the man was saying. "My pianist cut his thumb, so he can't play tonight. My trumpet player's gotten lost in Trump Tower, my drummer's dog ate her drumsticks, and my bass player—well, basically, he's boring. And to top it all off, the club is *crowded* tonight!"

"No problem," Herbie exclaimed. "We happen to be the Penguin Quartet, the world's best jazz band, and we'd love to help you out."

That night, the Penguin Quartet played the coolest jazz anyone had ever heard. The audience went wild with joy. People even danced on the tables!

The news about the Penguin Quartet spread across the entire world.

The jazz clubs begged for a chance to book a show with Charlie, Miles, Max, and Herbie. Everyone wanted to see the amazing musical penguins.

One day the penguins got a phone call from a television network. The Penguin Quartet was invited to guest star on a talk show!

It's not every day that penguins appear on TV, so of course they wanted to look their very best.

At first, everything went well. But suddenly, right in the middle of their interview, they heard a tiny "crack." The eggs were beginning to hatch!

"We have to get home!" Miles shouted.

The penguins rushed out of the studio and jumped into a taxicab. The taxi zoomed to the airport as fast as a race car.

"Come back soon!" shouted the crowd in the street.

"You can count on it!" Herbie said.

On their way home, they flew over
the ocean once more. Far, far away,
they could see a flock of dots—very fat dots!
The penguin moms, full of fish and looking very
satisfied, were heading back to the South Pole too.

"There's no place like home," said Max, who longed
to roll in the snow again.

"You said it," Charlie
agreed. "Our jazz tour
was fun, but even Mr.
Waldorf's place isn't as
cool as the South Pole."

YUM!

When all the penguins got home, they threw a huge party. They were awfully happy to see each other again. The penguin moms were happy to see the dads, and the penguin dads were happy to see the moms. And both the dads and the moms were happy to see the penguin babies when they crawled out of the eggs at last.

But the penguin babies were the happiest of them all, because they got to see all that snow—*and* their dads, *and* their moms—for the very first time.

"It's too bad you had to stand around here freezing your poor wings off," said the penguin moms, "while we were off gobbling up fish."

"Well," Herbie said with a sly little smile, "it wasn't all that bad." He grinned at the rest of the Penguin Quartet. "I'm even looking forward to next year!"

Charlie's friend Cynthia,
a flight attendant

Favorite
fishing hole

SEAFOOD SHANTY

4 FISH CHOWDERS
1 FILLET OF FLOUNDER $
12 FISH STICKS $1
1 FISHTAIL $6
9 COD LIVER OILS $9.
TOTAL $27.0

                        $68.00

Best Fish in the Big Apple
Seafood Shanty • 5th Avenue
New York

Tarzan?

Miles visits the
Statue of Liberty

Self-portrait
by Max →

Herbie chats with
the press after
a show

ISBN 0-439-10401-7

Text copyright © 1998 by Peter Arrhenius.
Illustrations copyright © 1998 by Ingela Peterson.
First published in Sweden in 1996 by Bokfölaget Natur och Kultur, Stockholm,
under the title *Pingvinkvartetten*.
All rights reserved.
Published by Scholastic Inc., 555 Broadway, New York, NY 10012,
by arrangement with Carolrhoda Books, Inc.
SCHOLASTIC and associated logos are trademarks and/or registered
trademarks of Scholastic Inc.

12 11 10 9 8 7 6 5 4 3 2 1   9/9 0 1 2 3 4/0

Printed in the U.S.A.   14

First Scholastic printing, December 1999